D0835574

When there's trouble, Spider-Man isn't far away. So when the Vulture steals the famous diamond, the Demon's Eye, Spider-Man goes into action fast. He knows the diamond has strange powers, and it mustn't be allowed to fall into the wrong hands.

British Library Cataloguing in Publication Data
Sharp, Mike
    The Demon's eye.
    I. Title   II. Davies, Robin, *1950-*   III. Series
823.914 [J]
    ISBN 0-7214-1336-6

First edition

Published by Ladybird Books Ltd Loughborough Leicestershire UK
Ladybird Books Inc Auburn Maine 04210 USA

© Copyright 1990 Marvel Entertainment Group, Inc. All rights reserved.
Spider-Man and all prominent characters and the distinctive likenesses thereof are trademarks of Marvel Entertainment Group, Inc. and are used with permission. No part of this publication may be reproduced, stored in a retrieval system, or transmitted in any form or by any means, electronic, mechanical, photo-copying, recording or otherwise, without the prior consent of the copyright owner.

Printed in England (3)

the AMAZING SPIDER-MAN®

THE DEMON'S EYE

by MIKE SHARP
illustrated by ROBIN DAVIES

Ladybird Books

"I want Spider-Man behind bars!"
barked J. Jonah Jameson at Peter Parker
and his friend, Joy Mercado. "When he
steps out of line, the *Daily Bugle* must be
the first to print the story."

"But Spider-Man isn't a crook,"
protested Joy.

"What do you youngsters know about crooks?" snapped Jameson. "And I want photographs, Parker."

"I'll...er...try," muttered Peter.

"Well, don't just stand around here, then!"

"No sir, Mr Jameson," said Peter, as he and Joy left the office.

"Do you think Spider-Man is a crook?" asked Joy.

"No more than you or I," said Peter. "But I do know a story we can cover..."

A crowd had gathered at the city museum.

"Today you will witness the unveiling

of the mysterious 'Demon's Eye'," announced the Swami.

There was a gasp from the crowd as the Holy Man revealed a huge glistening diamond. At the back of the hall however Peter felt his spider-sense buzz wildly.

The next moment, a figure smashed through the window with a mighty crash, and flew straight for the diamond. It was the Vulture! He aimed his sonic ray gun and a deafening wail knocked the guards to the floor.

"Quick, Peter, take a photograph!" shouted Joy over the din. But when she turned to speak to him he had disappeared.

The Vulture snatched the jewel and soared up and out of the window, laughing wickedly.

Peter had found an empty room where he pulled off his street clothes to reveal his secret identity. Seconds later Spider-Man leapt into the hall and swung out through the window in pursuit of the Vulture.

"Great!" thought Joy. "First the Vulture steals the 'Demon's Eye', then Spider-Man chases him – and we don't get a single photograph! Where *is* Peter when you really need him?"

"Now that I have the gem and all its power, the world will hear more of the Vulture," sneered the villain as he glided away from the museum. He glanced back and suddenly caught sight of Spider-Man, hot on his trail.

"So you think you are a match for the Vulture, eh?"

He swerved sharply, and slashed at Spider-Man's web to send him tumbling towards the earth.

"It's not going to be *that* easy," said Spider-Man, as he fired his web-shooters and snared the Vulture's ankle.

As Spider-Man hauled himself up, the Vulture flew higher above the city. Then he turned, towing Spider-Man down into a deadly nosedive. Spider-Man shot his web and swung to safety on a wall. But the Vulture had already pulled out of his dive and he fired his sonic ray. Spider-Man fell from the wall, stunned. By the time he picked himself up from the ground, the Vulture was a speck in the distance.

"'Web-slinger in diamond theft.' I'll put it on tomorrow's front page," said J. Jonah Jameson gleefully.

"But the Vulture stole the 'Demon's Eye'," said Joy.

"They were probably in it together," snapped Jameson.

"I'm sure you're wrong," said Joy nervously. "Spider-Man was trying to stop

the Vulture from stealing the gem and using its power. The Swami said that it transforms the light of sunrise into a laser beam."

"Mumbo-jumbo!" snarled Jameson. "And where's Parker with those photographs?"

"Er…" Joy tried to think up an excuse – without success!

Spider-Man had been
hunting all night for the
Vulture. Now the clouds were
beginning to burn deep
red as the sun rose. The
task seemed hopeless;
the city was huge with
many places to hide.

Then he saw the bright glitter of the
famous gem at the top of a disused
water tower. Below it was the distant but
unmistakable silhouette of the Vulture.

Spider-Man started to move fast in that
direction.

The Vulture's eye glowed as bright as the jewel as he dreamed of evil power.

"With this gem, I will have all the power of the sun's rays at my command. I will rule the land as well as the skies," he cackled triumphantly.

Suddenly the 'Eye' went black. A thick coating of webbing had blocked out the light.

"Spider-Man!" shrieked the Vulture.

"Got it in one, bird-brain!" said Spider-Man, swinging onto the tower.

The Vulture pulled out his sonic ray and flew at Spider-Man. But this time spider-sense came to Spider-Man's rescue, and he sprayed webbing over the muzzle of the gun.

He leapt on the Vulture as he sped
towards him, keeping clear of the wicked
talons that tried to claw at his throat.

Below, people stood amazed at the two
figures battling in mid-air.

Suddenly Spider-Man pulled free,
dropping onto a rooftop.

"Hah! Had enough, Spider-Man?"
sneered the Vulture.

But Spider-Man had felt his spider-sense buzz. The gem was still catching the sun's rays, and he had to shield his eyes as a brilliant flash burst from the jewel.

The Vulture shrieked, dazzled by the light. Spider-Man quickly caught him in

a web, swung him round and sent him crashing through a window.

When the villain came to, he was tightly bound in a cocoon of webbing.

"Well," thought Spider-Man, "that about wraps this case up."

"Here are some photographs of the Vulture being taken to prison, Mr Jameson," said Peter, back at the *Daily Bugle*. "And Spider-Man told me to return the 'Demon's Eye' to its rightful owner, so we're going over to the museum now."

"A thousand blessings," said the Swami a few minutes later, when they handed over the famous gem.

"So all this time you *were* chasing after Spider-Man and the Vulture to get photographs," said Joy as they went back to work.

"That's right," said Peter with a grin. "I got a bird's-eye view of the whole thing."